The Old Animals' Forest Band
First published in English by Tara Publishing

Copyright © 2008 Tara Publishing
For the text: Sirish Rao
For the illustrations: Durga Bai

For this edition:
Tara Publishing Ltd., U.K. <www.tarabooks.com/uk>
and
Tara Publishing, India <www.tarabooks.com>

Design: Rathna Ramanathan
Production: C. Arumugam

ISBN: 978-81-86211-45-8

The Old Animals' Forest Band

Sirish Rao

Durga Bai

TARA PUBLISHING

In a little village near the forest was a man who had a dog. The dog was old and spent most of his time sleeping.

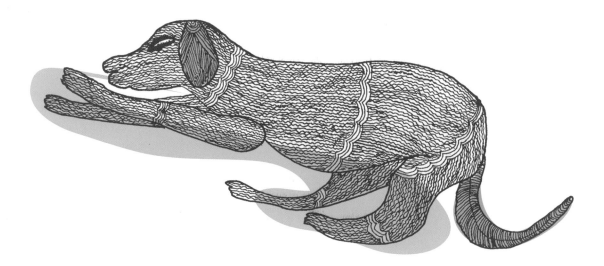

One day, a stranger came to the gate, and the dog didn't bark and warn his master as he used to.

'You're no use anymore! Off you go!' said the man, and threw the dog out.

The poor dog was sad and lay down outside the gate of the house.

Along came a cow, chewing cud and walking slowly. 'Why the long face?' she asked when she saw the dog so sad.

So the dog told the cow his story.

'Oooooohhh!' said the cow. 'Sounds just like my story.'

'I used to belong to a farmer. He milked me every day, and raised all his six children on my milk. But now that I'm old and there's no milk in me anymore, he threw me out. That was last week. I've been wandering around since then.'

The dog said to the cow, 'What now, cow?'

'Well there's two of us, so at least we have company. Let's go to the forest outside the village. Maybe we can find somewhere to stay…'

And the two started walking to the forest, chatting about their lives.

On the way, they saw a donkey standing in the middle of the road, crying loudly.

'What's the problem?' asked the dog and the cow speaking at the same time, since they had already become good friends.

'The washerman threw me out,' moaned the donkey. 'I carried his washing to the river and back for years. But I'm not that young anymore and he says I'm too slow. I've nowhere to go!'

'Same story again!' the dog and the cow said. 'Join us! We're going to start a new life in the forest.'

So the three of them walked along, talking. It was turning dark and they were near the edge of the forest when they heard the loud call of a rooster from a treetop.

'It's not morning!' all three cried.

'Sorry!' the rooster said. 'I'm so old I can't tell day from night anymore. That's why my mistress threw me out...'

'These humans are all the same!' said the three friends, and asked the rooster to go along with them.

Soon they were deep in the forest. It was very dark and they were a little frightened. Suddenly, the dog pricked his ears up and said, 'I hear something!'

So the rooster climbed a small tree and squawked, 'Over there, I see a light!'

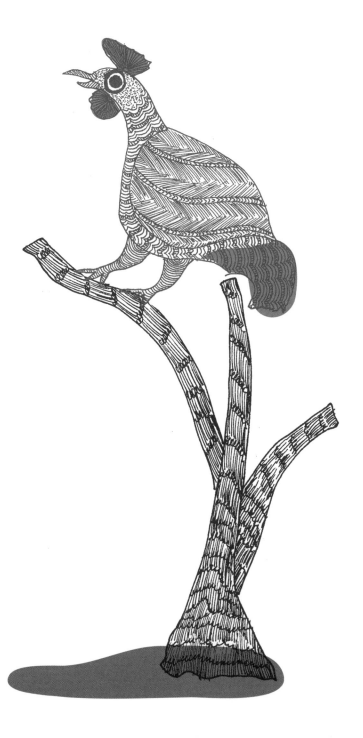

And so the four walked towards the light until they came to a clearing with an old hut in the middle of it. There was a light on inside, and they could hear voices, but they were too frightened to enter. 'Let's peep in!' the cow said and went closer, but the window was closed.

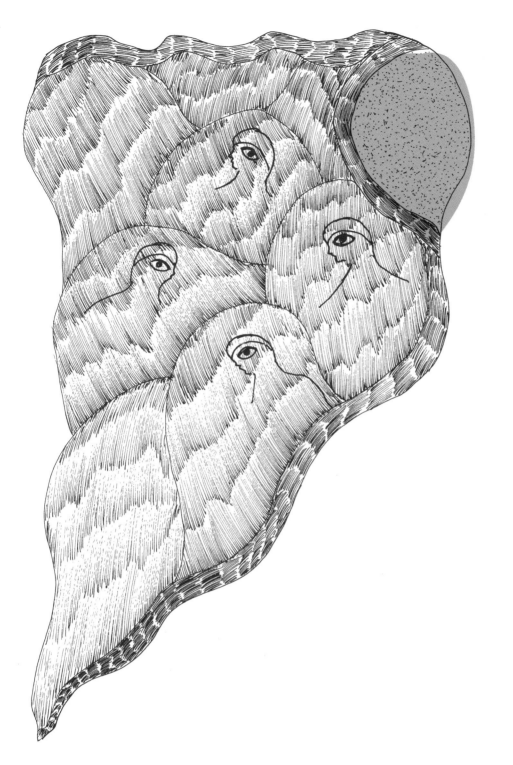

Then the rooster had an idea. 'See that crack in the roof where the light shows through? Let's stand one on top of another and I'll peep through it.' So they just about balanced on each other and the rooster managed to peep through.

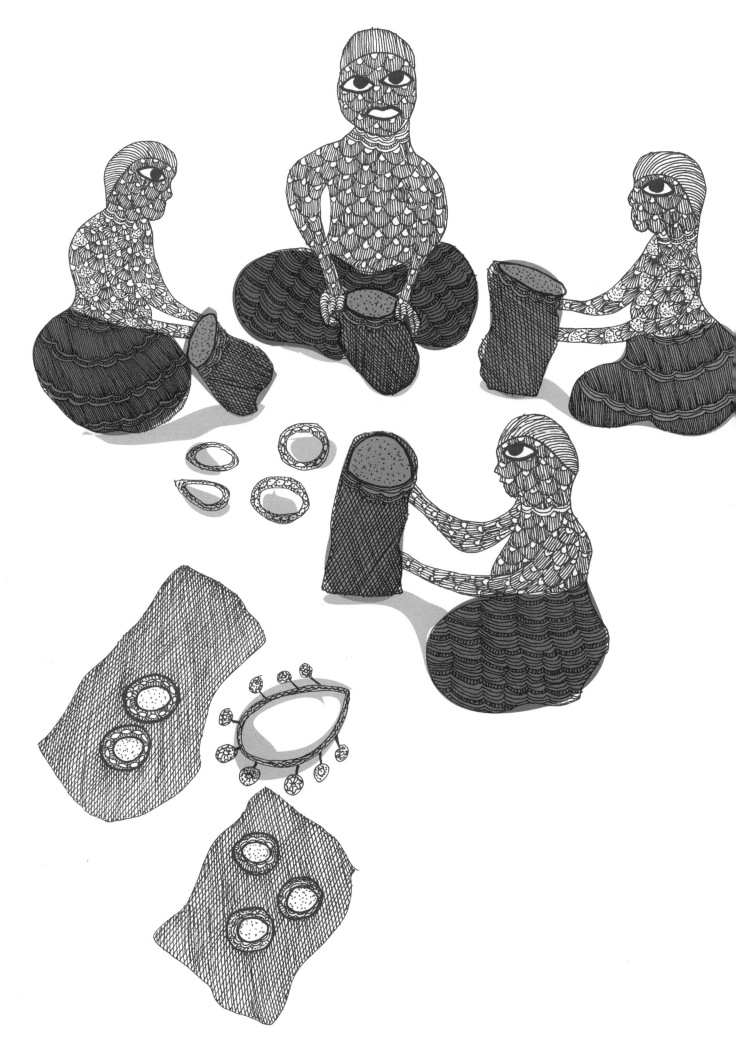

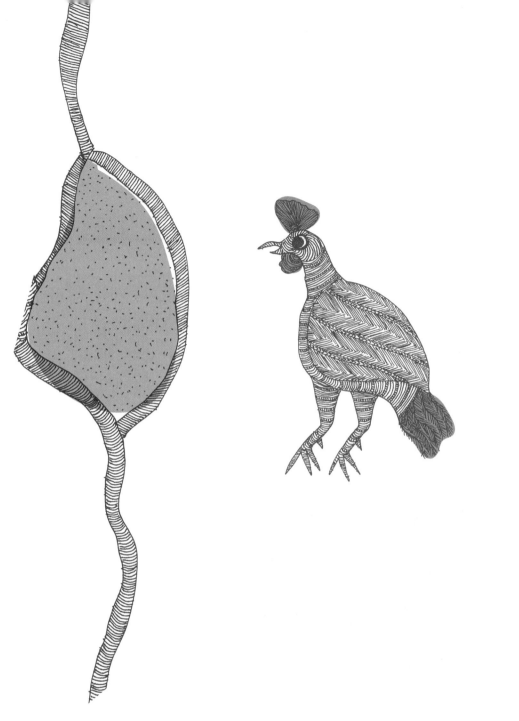

There were four men sitting inside, surrounded by bags of gold and jewels that they were counting. They were fighting with each other about sharing the gold.

'Thieves!' whispered the rooster to his friends. 'What shall we do?'

'I'm frightened,' said the donkey from below.

'Let's not be scared. Let's scare them!' said the dog.

'How?' said the rooster. 'We're old and slow!'

'Let's make a noise!' said the dog. 'Can any of you sing?'

'NO!' said the donkey and the cow who had never sung in their lives.

'Good! Neither can I!' said the dog. 'Now sing as loudly as you can.'

So they sang as loudly as they could, all together.

And it sounded terrible.

The rooster crowed,
'Cock-a-doodle-dooooo.'

And the dog yowled,
'Bowwww-wowwww, bow-woooow.'

And the donkey brayed,
'He-hah, he-haaaaah...'

And the cow bellowed,
'Moo-mooooo...'

The sound they made together was so loud and so awful that the thieves thought the worst monster on earth was coming to eat them. They ran away from the hut as fast as they could, leaving all the jewels and gold behind.

Very pleased with their work, the animals entered the hut and made themselves comfortable.

Meanwhile, the terrible song of the animals had reached as far as the village, and woken everybody up. Everyone rushed to the forest and came to the hut to see what the problem was.

When they came in, the people saw the bags of gold and jewels that the thieves had left behind.

'These are the things that were stolen from our village!' the people cried. 'Ha ha! We've got them back, thanks to these animals!'

'That's my dog!' said a man, coming forward.

'And my cow!' said another. 'My donkey!' said a third. 'So that's where my rooster went!' said a woman.

All the villagers praised the animals, and so the masters tried to take them back home with them.

But this time, it was the animals who threw their masters out. 'Go away!' They all shouted together and chased their masters out of the hut. 'We don't need you anymore either. We've got a house, we've got each other, and we've got a plan!'

So the masters ran back to the village, wondering what plan the animals had.

And the plan?

The animals had enjoyed their singing so much, they decided to call themselves the Old Animals' Forest Band. They stayed on happily in the hut in the forest and gave loud performances every day.

And danced to their own music.